DOCTOR COSMO'S SPACE SPECTACULAR

KAI YANG

ISBN 979-8-89133-622-3

This is Sam.
He's a fine young man.
He likes to learn
as much as he can.

"I'm so bored!" cried Sam,
as he put on a sock.
"I'm going to go
outside for a walk!"

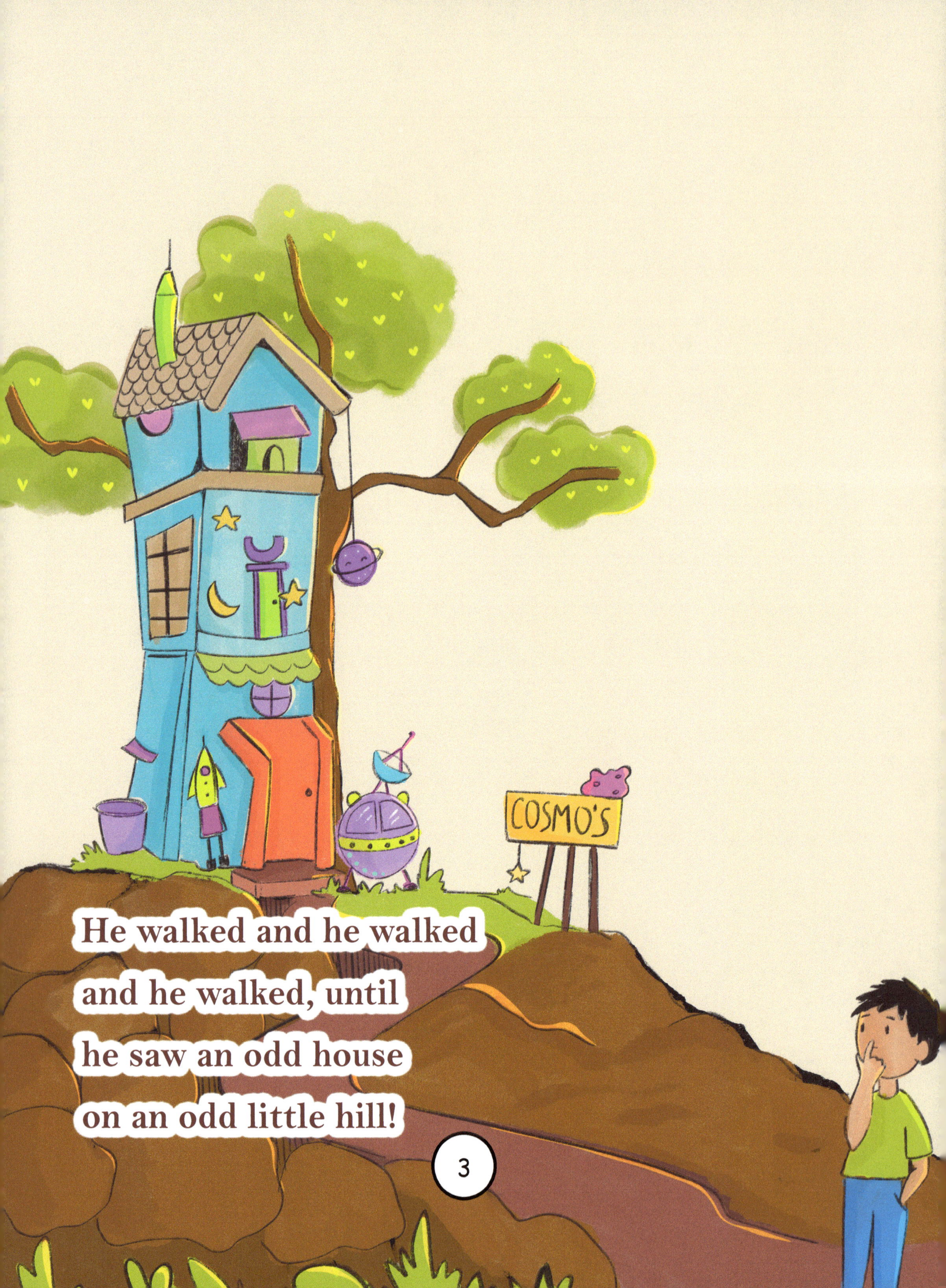

He walked and he walked
and he walked, until
he saw an odd house
on an odd little hill!

3

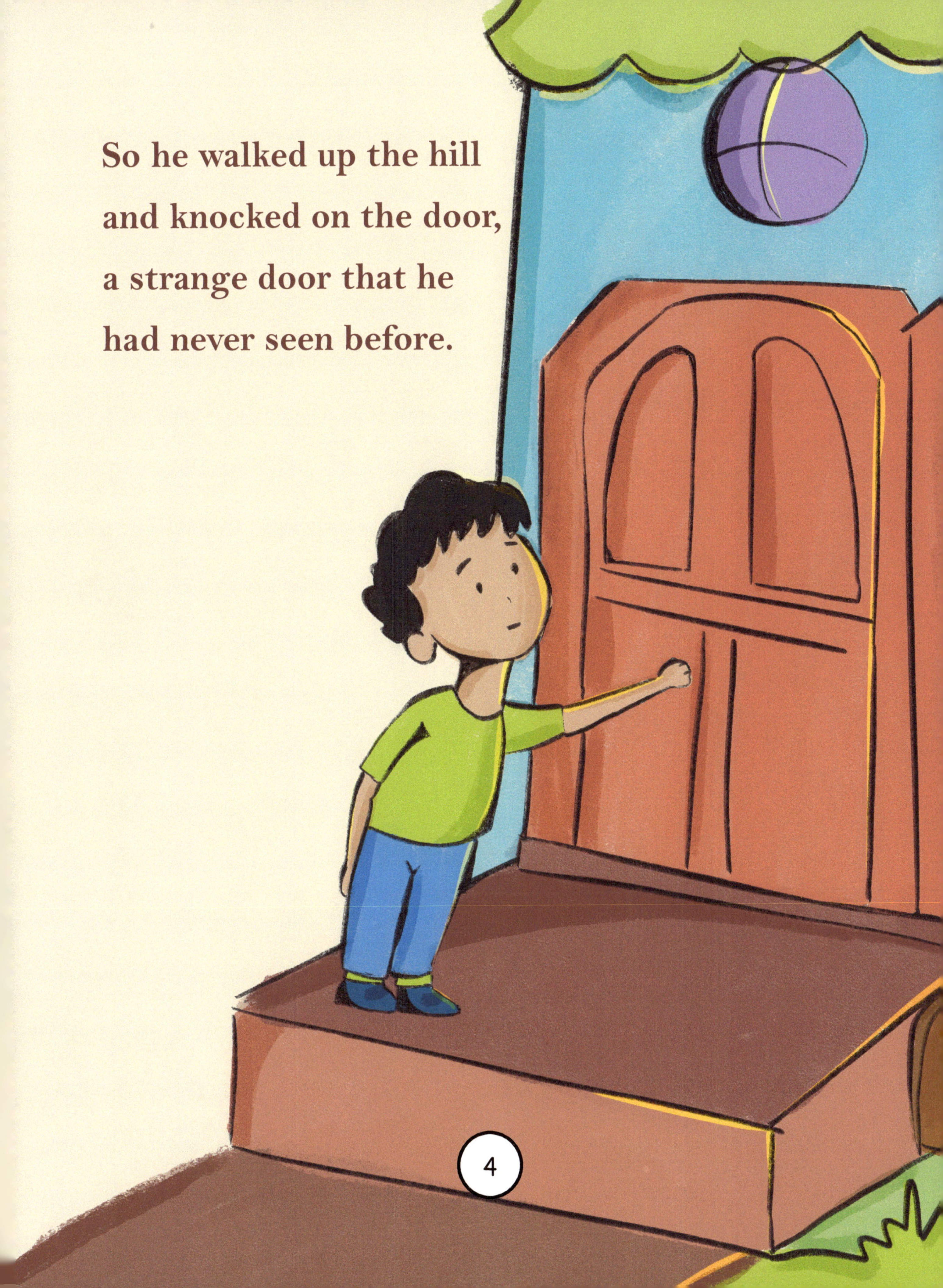

So he walked up the hill
and knocked on the door,
a strange door that he
had never seen before.

The door creaked open,
and Sam let out a cry.
Out popped a figure
with a twinkle in his eye.

He had wild, silver hair
and a long, droopy nose,
and he was dressed in bright blue
from his head to his toes.

"Welcome, dear Sam,
to this wonderful place!
I'm Doctor Cosmo,
the professor of space!"

6

With a fizz and a spark,
they stepped through the door.
To a room full of wonders,
and books on the floor.
The walls of the house
were as dark as the night,
and the ceiling was painted
with stars of pure light.

"We're blasting off, Sam,
Come along with me!
There's so much to do,
so much to see!"

With the press of a button,
the house started to fly.
Sam clutched at his stomach
as they zoomed through the sky.

"We're off to explore
the great space up above.
Hold on tight, my friend,
for an adventure you'll love!"

As they whizzed through the air,
Cosmo turned with a grin.
"We've made it to space.
Let our journey begin!"

"We'll visit the planets,
each one so unique.
Look, we're approaching
the first one as we speak!"

"Now this is Mercury, so close to the sun.
It spins oh so fast, and it's a whole lot of fun!
Its surface is rocky, what a marvelous sight!
It's hot in the day and freezing cold at night!"

"Next up, Venus shines with a golden hue,
its sulfur clouds swirl like a magical brew.
Even hotter than Mercury, and so odd, if I may,
a planet so odd that it spins the other way!"

"Third is the Earth, our beautiful home,
with so many creatures, we're never alone.
A world full of life, on land and at sea,
a world full of wonders, for you and for me!"

Then onward they zipped to Mars red and grand,
with deserts and dunes, and rust-colored sand.
"On Mars," said Cosmo, "You'd better beware!
The dust storms will sweep you into the air!"

"Jupiter, the giant, the king of the skies,
with swirling gas clouds, it hides a surprise!
At Jupiter's heart lies the Great Red Spot,
a churning red storm that blazes red hot!"

"Saturn, oh Saturn, such beautiful rings,
they've got to be one of my favorite things!
So delicate and thin, it may come as a shock,
to learn that the rings are made of ice and rock!"

"Uranus is special—it spins on its sides,
the coldest planet, with blue-green tides.
Let's not stay too long, Sam, with a skip and a hop,
we'll move on to Neptune, our very last stop!"

"Neptune is the farthest, with a brilliant blue face,
drifting in the darkest depths of space.
The last of the planets, now this marks the end,
and it's time to go home, Sam, my marvelous friend."

So they zoomed back to Earth,
passing comets in flight,
Sam counted the planets, each one
shining bright.
One planet, two planets, three
planets, four,
five planets, six planets, seven and
one more!

Eight exciting planets, but
Sam wanted more still!

He turned to ask Cosmo, as
they landed on the hill.

"Hey Doctor Cosmo, is there
more for me to see?"

"Why, of course!" replied
Cosmo, jumping up in glee.

"But come again tomorrow, that's
all I have today.

Bring your friends along, and we'll
explore the Milky Way!"

So Sam said goodbye to Cosmo,
and dusted off his shoe.

He walked home feeling happy that
he had learned something new!

So when you're feeling bored, or just looking for a thrill,

pay a visit to the odd little house on the hill,

to explore the universe, such a spectacular place,

with Doctor Cosmo, the professor of space!